ONE FINE TRADE

retold by
Bobbi Miller
illustrated by **Will Hillenbrand**

Holiday House / New York

AUTHOR'S NOTE

This folktale is based on an old folk song. A variation can be found in Moritz Jagendorf's *Folkstories of the South* (New York: Vanguard Press, 1972).

ACKNOWLEDGMENTS

Without their guidance, support, and friendship, I would not have been able to write my story: Eric Kimmel, guru; Marion Dane Bauer, mentor and friend; Regina Griffin, editora extraordinairia; and the excellent teaching and support of the Writing for Children and Young Adults master's program at Vermont College and Center for the Study of Children's Literature master's program, Simmons College.

Text copyright © 2009 by Bobbi Miller
Illustrations copyright © 2009 by Will Hillenbrand
All Rights Reserved
Printed and Bound in China
The text typeface is Oldavai.
The illustrations were done with ink and pencil on vellum. These elements were
scanned, digitally manipulated, and printed on watercolor paper. Colored pencil
and gouache were then added to the final art.
www.holidayhouse.com
First Edition
1 3 5 7 9 10 8 6 4 2

Library of Congress Cataloging-in-Publication Data
Miller, Bobbi.
One fine trade / retold by Bobbi Miller ; illustrated by Will Hillenbrand. — 1st ed.
p. cm.
Summary: Georgy Piney Woods, the best peddler who ever lived, makes several trades
so his daughter can buy a wedding dress.
ISBN-13: 978-0-8234-1836-7 (hardcover)
[1. Folklore—United States. 2. Peddlers and peddling—Folklore.]
I. Hillenbrand, Will, ill. II. Georgy Piney-Woods Peddler. English. III. Title.
PZ8.1.M6122On 2008
398.2—dc22
[E]
2007025493

To Becca,
"Always for you, child mine."
—B. M.

For Peter and Katie,
who wanted a world full of windows,
all opportunities. Passages to be
experienced bravely,
honestly, and joyfully . . .
one fine trade.
—W. H.

GEORGY PINEY WOODS was a fine peddler, the finest who ever lived! One gloriously fine morning his daughter, Georgianne, said, "Dadaw, my wedding day is a-coming soon enough. Can you trade my rail-skinny horse for a shiny silver dollar that I might buy me a pretty new dress?"

"Always for you, child mine," said Georgy Piney Woods. "Quick as greased lightning, I'll bring you the shiniest silver dollar."

Down the road he went, a-riding the rail-skinny horse.

The road twisted this way and that, up hill and down dale.

All around, catbirds were a-mewing, crows were a-cawing and herons a-squawking.

Along came . . .

a farmer, leading
a fat brown cow.

"How-do!" said Georgy Piney Woods. "Trade you this rail-skinny horse, I will, if you have a shiny silver dollar."

"Got no silver dollar," said the farmer. His fat brown cow mooooed. "I'm in mighty need of a horse. I'll trade you my cow."

"And one fine trade it is!" said Georgy Piney Woods. And down the road he marched, leading the fat brown cow.

As he rode down the winding road, it gave way to a meadow.

All around, daisies were a-dancing and clovers were a-swaying.

Along came...

an old woman, leading
an old hound dog.

"How-do!" said Georgy Piney Woods.
"Trade you my fat brown cow, I will,
if you have a shiny silver dollar."
    "Got no silver dollar," said the old woman.
Her old hound dog hooowled. "I can surely
use a cow. I'll trade you my old hound dog."

"And one fine trade it is!" said Georgy Piney Woods. And off he trotted down the road, that old hound dog a-wagging at his heels.

The meadow gave way to a swamp. All around, gators were a-thundering and otters a-splashing. Then the swamp gave way to deep deep woods. All around, bobcats were a-yowling and black bears were a-prowling.

Along came...

a hunter, who was swinging
a cypress stick.

"How-do! How-do!" said Georgy Piney Woods. "Trade you this ol'
hound dog, I will, if you have a shiny silver dollar."

"Got no silver dollar," said the hunter. He spun the stick—*SWISH*. "But
I could surely use an old hound dog. I'll trade you my stick."

"And one fine trade it is!" said Georgy Piney Woods. Off he sauntered
down the road, a-swinging that stick in stride.

Along slithered . . .

a giant snake,
a-shaking his rattle.

"How-do!" said Georgy Piney Woods. "Trade you my stick, I will, if you have a shiny silver dollar."

"Got no silver dollar," the snake hissed. "I gotss sharp teeth full of poison. I gotss a hankering to takess that stick of yourss and payss you not one dime!"

Now, that giant snake lunged at the cypress stick. He sank his fangs deep deep into the wood. So deep, in fact, he couldn't shake them loose. Quick the peddler swung the stick round and round. Off flew the giant snake so far and wide, he's not been seen in the deep deep woods again.

Wouldn't ya know that the cypress stick was so filled with the snake's venom, it began to swell. That stick swelled 'til it stood as big as a tree. Yep, indeedy, it swelled as big as two trees.

It swelled as big as three trees!

It so happens, along came . . . .

a railroad man.

"How-do!" said Georgy Piney Woods. "Trade you my giant cypress stick, I will, if you have a shiny silver dollar."

"I got a shiny silver dollar," said the railroad man. "I'm in need of your giant cypress stick."

"And one fine trade it is!" said Georgy Piney Woods.

Said the railroad man, "Now, I don't carry such a shiny silver dollar in my pocket. Thieves are about, you know. Give me your stick, and tomorrow I will bring you the silver dollar."

You bet Georgy Piney Woods gave him that stick.

The railroad man chopped the stick into three hundred and three railroad ties. He laid them down along the railroad bed.

It began to rain. It rained all night, rained so hard that it washed the poison from the three hundred and three railroad ties. The ties shrank smaller and smaller, until they were small as walking sticks. The rain poured harder, and the sticks grew smaller. Soon they were no more than toothpicks.

With the bright morning sun, Georgy Piney Woods came a-calling
to pick up his shiny silver dollar. The railroad man gathered the
toothpicks all in one hand.

"Look here at my giant cypress stick now!" he shouted.
"Why, I have no need of toothpicks!"

Right then the railroad man's wife came
a-running to see what
all the shouting was about.

"How-do! How-do! How did ya know I'm in need
of toothpicks," sang she, quite pleased. "And aren't
these very fine ones at that."

The railroad man's wife paid Georgy Piney Woods
one shiny silver dollar for the toothpicks.

And Georgianne bought the pretty new dress for her wedding.

Wouldn't ya know, then Georgianne asked, "Dadaw, I surely do need a pretty new veil to go with my pretty new dress for my wedding day. Can you trade my little red hen for a shiny silver dime that I may buy such a pretty veil?"

"Always for you, child mine," said Georgy Piney Woods with a smile. "Quick as bees buzz, I will bring you a shiny silver dime." And off he went.

But wouldn't ya know, he had one more fine trade. Quick as cats pounce he traded his dandy nanny goat for a pretty gold wedding ring. "And one fine trade it is!" said Georgy Piney Woods, the finest peddler who ever lived.

Pretty CHAPeL
...and they all lived...
HAPPILY·EVER·AFTER.